To Mum (and all mums everywhere!) ~ D.O'C.

For Ninetta, Regina, Anna and Rosy. ~ F.G.

HarperCollins
PUBLISHERS
Since 1817

First published in paperback in Great Britain by HarperCollins Children's Books in 2017

1 3 5 7 9 10 8 6 4 2

ISBN: 978-0-00-810025-4

HarperCollins Children's Books is a division of HarperCollins Publishers Ltd.

Text copyright © David O'Connell 2017
Illustrations copyright © Francesca Gambatesa 2017

Visit our website at: www.harpercollins.co.uk

Printed in China

When I'm a Mummy Like You!

When I'm a Mummy Like You!

David O'Connell
Francesca Gambatesa

HarperCollins *Children's Books*

I want to be a mum like you, Mum!
I want to be a grown-up
RIGHT NOW!

You make it
look simple
so it can't be
that hard –

Please, please, PLEASE
can you tell me how?

I want to do the stuff that grown-ups do
When I'm a Mummy like you!

Being a mum is not easy,
With so many things to be done.

From breakfast to bedtime
I'm rushed off my feet –

There's always some
place else to run!

Being a Mummy is lots of fun, too,
But that's all because
I have you.

No one can cook like you, Mum! Everything you serve up is a **winner**.

From frying to baking it turns out **just right** –
I can't **wait** to find out what's for dinner!

I want to do the stuff that grown-ups do
When I'm a Mummy like you!

My cooking is **not** always perfect,
No matter how much I take care.

But whatever the weather,
wherever we are,
The **best** meals are
those that we **share**.

Being a Mummy is lots of fun, too,
But that's all because I have you.

I wish I could keep fit with you, Mum!
You run and you catch and you throw.

You're always the best, whatever the game –
You're the number one Mummy I know!

I want to do the stuff that grown-ups do
When I'm a Mummy like you!

It's **great** being out in the open
and running all over the place,
But the **best** games of all are the ones played with **you**...

Look out – I'm about to give chase!

Being a Mummy is lots of fun, too,
But that's all because I have you.

Can I get dressed up
just like you, Mum?

I **love** all the clothes
that you choose.

You go off to work
and you take on the **world** –

I wish I could walk
in your shoes!

I want to do the stuff that grown-ups do
When I'm a Mummy like you!

Have I remembered
my handbag?

And **where** are my
phone and my keys?

I'd rather stay home
on the sofa with you –
Feasting on crackers
and cheese!

Being a Mummy is lots of fun, too,
But that's all because I have you.

I wish I was **fearless**
like you, Mum,
And not scared of the
monsters at night.

You always make
everything better,

You always make
everything right.

I want to do the stuff
that grown-ups do
When I'm a
Mummy like you!

Night time can sometimes be frightening –
Even I use the bedclothes to hide.
But no matter the worry, no matter the fear
I'll **always** *be there by your side.*

Being a Mummy is lots of fun, too,
But that's all because I have you.

If I **grow up** to be a mum like you, Mum,
You'll **still** be my mummy, won't you?

I'll **always** be Mum,
that won't ever change...

And you'll still be my little one *too.*